For Danielle, Corrine, and Zachary.
Sorry I hogged the Golden Grahams. —M.M.

For Clay, who always makes room —M.P.

THIS IS A BORZOI BOOK PUBLISHED BY ALFRED A. KNOPF

Text copyright © 2022 by Megan Maynor
Jacket art and interior illustrations copyright © 2022 by Micah Player

All rights reserved. Published in the United States by Alfred A. Knopf, an imprint of
Random House Children's Books, a division of Penguin Random House LLC, New York.

Knopf, Borzoi Books, and the colophon are registered trademarks of
Penguin Random House LLC.

Visit us on the Web! rhcbooks.com

Educators and librarians, for a variety of teaching tools, visit us at RHTeachersLibrarians.com

Library of Congress Cataloging-in-Publication Data
Names: Maynor, Megan, author. | Player, Micah, illustrator.
Title: Not enough lollipops / by Megan Maynor ; illustrations by Micah Player.
Description: First edition. | New York : Alfred A. Knopf, 2022. | Audience: Ages 4–7. |
Summary: Alice wins a wagon full of lollipops in a school raffle, but no one is sure if there
are enough for everyone to have one.
Identifiers: LCCN 2020022573 (print) | LCCN 2020022574 (ebook) | ISBN 978-0-593-37256-2 (hardcover) |
ISBN 978-0-593-37257-9 (library binding) | ISBN 978-0-593-37258-6 (ebook)
Subjects: CYAC: Sharing—Fiction. | Candy—Fiction.
LCC PZ7.1.M388 No 2022 (print) | LCC PZ7.1.M388 (ebook) |
DDC [E]—dc23

The text of this book is set in 14-point Acre Regular.
The illustrations were created digitally in Adobe Fresco.
Book design by Nicole Gastonguay

MANUFACTURED IN CHINA
January 2022
10 9 8 7 6 5 4 3 2 1

First Edition

RAFFLE TICKET
SIMON C.

RAFFLE TICKET
Mary B.

RAFFLE TICKET
STEPHANIE J.

RAFFLE TICKET
Benjamin C.

NOT ENOUGH LOLLIPOPS

by Megan Maynor

art by Micah Player

RAFFLE TICKET
LUCK

RAFFLE TICKET
Alice G.

RAFFLE TICKET
Jerome T.

ALFRED A. KNOPF
New York

The final prize in the school raffle was a basket of lollipops so big, the principal pulled it onstage in a wagon.

Alice and her friends held hands and closed their eyes to focus their luck. "And the winner is . . ."

The gym exploded with screaming and cheering.

AL-ICE! AL-ICE! AL-ICE!

Alice high-fived everyone on her way to the stage.

"Wow," she whispered.
The lollipops glowed
like gems.

Alice pulled the wagon through the crowd, and kids called out.

can I HAVE one, TOO?

Alice laughed. "Sure, if there are enough."

Alice walked faster, out the big doors and onto the playground. The wagon rattled behind her.

Kids jumped in front of Alice.

ALICE, PLEASE, I haven't had a LOLLIPOP since my last HAIRCUT.

YOU'RE my ONLY HOPE for CANDY till HALLOWEEN.

"Oh no," said Alice.
"Are you okay?"

Kids snuck up alongside Alice.

PSST. ALICE. SKIP the KINDERGARTNERS. they can't HANDLE lollipops. THEY'LL just DROP THEM in the DIRT.

"They will?" asked Alice.

PSST. ALICE. DON'T count the NEW KID. THIS PRIZE is for your REAL CLASSMATES—the ones WHO have BEEN HERE since the FIRST DAY of SCHOOL.

PSST. ALICE. SKIP the FIFTH GRADERS. THEY don't DESERVE lollipops. THEY always HOG the TIRE SWING.

"Real classmates?" asked Alice.

"They do . . . ," said Alice.

"**ENOUGH!**" yelled Alice. Everyone froze.
"This prize was a waste of luck." Alice glared at the lollipops.
They had lost their glow. "Maybe I should give it back."

"But how? How am I supposed to choose who can handle a lollipop? Or who deserves one? Or who counts?"

Alice paced in front of the wagon. The crowd pushed closer.

"What if . . . what if I *don't* choose? What if I say everyone can handle a lollipop? Everyone deserves one. Everyone counts."

but, ALICE, what if there AREN'T ENOUGH for EVERYONE?

"What if . . . there are?" asked Alice. "Let's give it a try. One apiece."

LINE starts HERE!

NO, line up BEHIND me!

I'M the FRONT of the LINE!

Alice climbed into the wagon.
"I AM THE FRONT OF THE LINE!
Line up HERE."

And they did.

The line twisted and turned around the playground,
a mix of sweet and sour faces.

Alice got to work. *Butterscotch, strawberry, pineapple, lime . . .*

YAY!

Some kids were happy to get a lollipop.

HEY...

Some were upset to get only one lollipop.

Alice kept going. *Raspberry,
fruit punch, root beer, grape . . .*

THIS is TAKING
FOREVER.
I have BUBBLE GUM
at HOME.

Some kids left the line.

Alice and her wagon were nearing the end.
Cream soda, sour apple, cotton candy, orange . . .
Would there be enough?

Alice handed a lollipop to the last
student in line, then reached into
the basket . . . and pulled out
one for herself.

"Cherry! My favorite!"

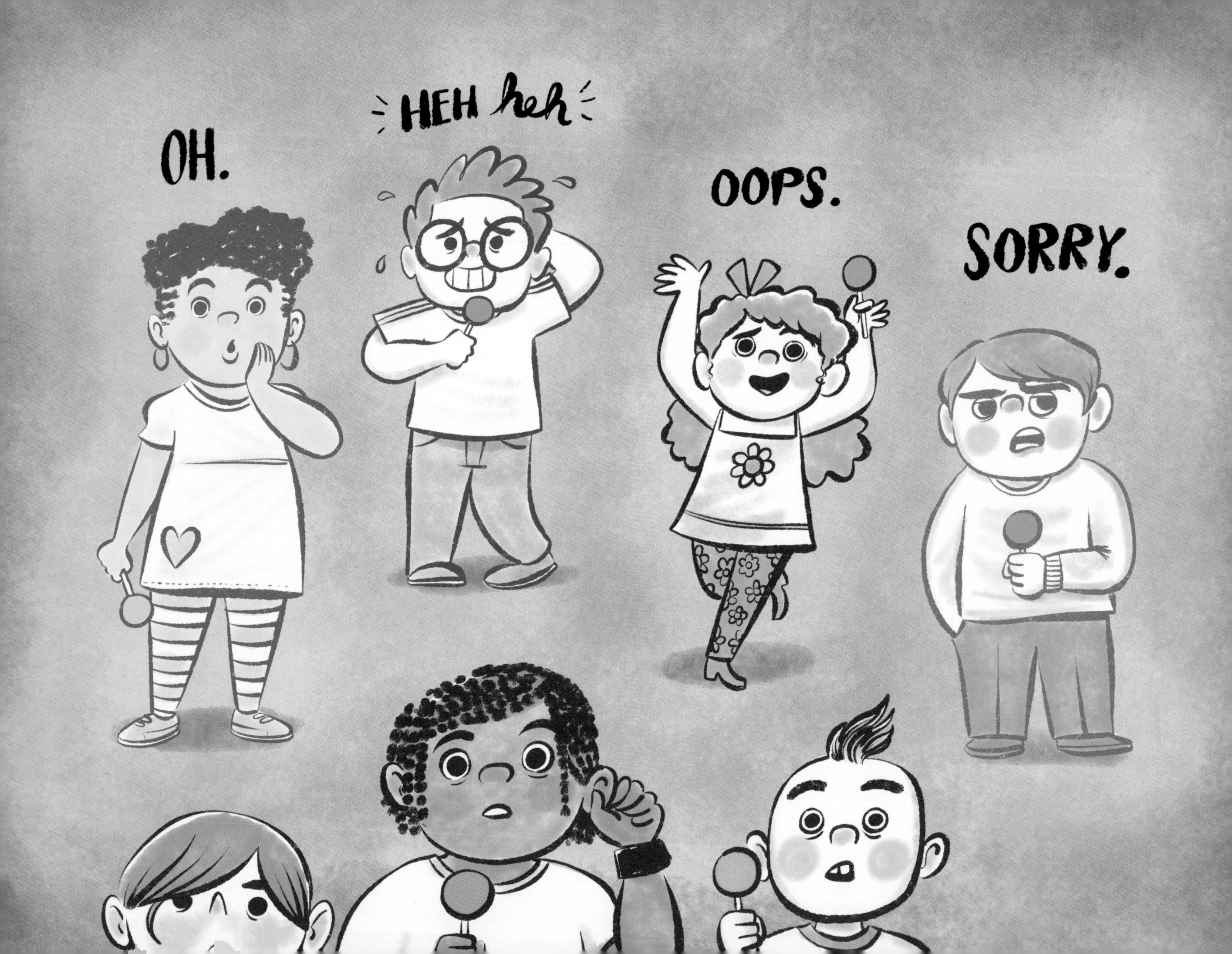
OH.
HEH heh
OOPS.
SORRY.

is your FOOT okay?

KINDERGARTNERS can handle LOTS of THINGS...

I used to be the NEW KID...

The lollipops glowed like gems again.

Then a first grader peeked into the wagon.

ALICE, what will you do WITH the EXTRAS?

"Oh no," said Alice.